Best Enemies
AGAIN

D1306925

KATHLEEN LEVERICH

Best Enemies AGAIN

Illustrated by Walter Lorraine

A TRUMPET CLUB SPECIAL EDITION

Published by The Trumpet Club
666 Fifth Avenue, New York, New York 10103

Text copyright © 1991 by Kathleen Leverich
Illustrations copyright © 1991 by Walter Lorraine

ISBN 0-440-84923-3

This edition published by arrangement with Greenwillow
Books, a division of William Morrow & Company, Inc.

Printed in the United States of America
February 1993

10 9 8 7 6 5 4 3 2 1
OPM

For
PRISCILLA
MOULTON

Contents

1 | Lemonade

That Friday afternoon Priscilla Robin left school feeling very cheerful. She had gotten an A on her book report. She had answered two difficult questions in science. Best of all, she had thought of the perfect place to sell lemonade. Starting Saturday, she would set up a stand at the top of Half-Mile Hill.

Priscilla pulled her old blue bike out of the school bike rack and climbed on. As she pedaled down

School Street, the sun felt warm on her back. The breeze felt cool on her face. She turned a corner. Half-Mile Hill rose straight ahead. Half-Mile Hill was the biggest hill on her way home. It was the biggest hill in the whole town. Priscilla pedaled hard to get a good start. She began the long, difficult ride to the top.

"*Wheii—wheii—wheiii,*" panted Priscilla. Her legs felt weak. Her mouth was dry. "*Wheii—wheii—wheiii.*" Pedaling was slow and hard, but if she stopped, she wouldn't be able to get started again. She'd have to walk her bike the rest of the way up. "*Wheii—wheii—wheiii.*" She could almost see the shady spot at the top where she'd be able to rest.

"Hey, you, Priscilla Robin Redbreast!"

Only one person would say Priscilla's name in that rude way. Only one person would interrupt someone trying to bicycle up Half-Mile Hill. Only one person lived in a house partway up the hill.

"Hey, Priscilla!"

Priscilla looked. Beside the road stood a curly-haired girl. Her pink and yellow sunsuit was covered with ruffles. Her pink and yellow sandals had ruffly pink and yellow flowers all over the straps. Only one person wore that many ruffles. Felicity. Felicity Doll.

"Look out! You've got a flat tire," cried Felicity.

Priscilla tottered. Her bike swerved. She scrambled off to check. "There's nothing wrong with my tires," she yelled. "You did that on purpose so I'd have to walk! *Wheii—wheii—wheiii.*" She couldn't stop panting.

Felicity looked concerned. "You've been pedaling hard. You must be thirsty. Would you like some of my cherry soda?" She held out a frosty glass.

Priscilla blinked. "I am thirsty. Thank you, I would." She reached for the glass—

"Too bad!" Felicity yanked it out of reach. While Priscilla watched, she gulped down every drop of the icy stuff. Then she crunched the ice.

Priscilla could almost taste that icy cold cube. She gripped her handlebars harder. "I may be thirsty now, but starting tomorrow, there'll be plenty of cold drinks on this hill!"

Felicity stopped chewing. She swallowed what was left of the ice. "Just what do you mean by that?"

Priscilla knew it was a mistake ever to tell Felicity

anything. But she was too excited to stop. "The top of this hill is the best place in town for a lemonade stand. Tomorrow I'm going to have one there."

Felicity looked at the quiet, shady spot at the top of the hill.

Priscilla said, "I'm going to charge ten cents for a small glass and twenty-five cents for a large one."

"Ten cents—?" said Felicity. "Twenty-five—?"

"Everyone who goes up this hill is thirsty. They'll all buy lemonade, and I'll make lots of money," said Priscilla. She could almost see the tired, thirsty people crowding around her stand.

"Money—?" Felicity frowned. She looked again at the quiet, shady spot at the top of the hill. "A lemonade stand—?"

Priscilla was going to answer, but Felicity wasn't talking to her. Felicity was talking to herself.

"You told who?" said Priscilla's big sister, Eve, that night at dinner.

"Whom," corrected Mrs. Robin. She spread her napkin in her lap. "You told whom. . . ."

"I told Felicity," said Priscilla.

"Wrrrrrouuu," whimpered Priscilla's dog, Pow-wow. He was waiting under the table in case anyone spilled food.

Eve looked serious. "Telling Felicity Doll about your lemonade stand was a big mistake."

Priscilla felt her stomach get knotty. Her palms began to sweat.

Mr. Robin said, "What harm could it do to tell Felicity?"

Priscilla said, "Yes, Eve, what harm?"

Eve shook her head. "I don't know yet. I do know that Felicity Doll is a real snake. Telling her anything, ever, is asking for trouble."

"I knew it," said Priscilla. She suddenly wasn't hungry.

"Nonsense," said Mrs. Robin. "By now Felicity has forgotten all about Priscilla's lemonade stand."

"Do you really think so?" Priscilla felt a little better.

Mrs. Robin said, "I'm sure of it. Who would like chutney with their fish?"

Priscilla's stomach relaxed. Her palms stopped sweating. She thought, Mom's right. What does Felicity care? She took a big helping of chutney and began to wonder just how many glasses of lemonade she would sell the next day.

The next morning Mr. Robin helped Priscilla load the big cooler into her wagon. Mrs. Robin helped her fill it with ice from the freezer. Eve helped her mix four big batches of lemonade in giant jars. Everyone helped arrange the jars in the cooler.

"Do you have enough cups?" said Mr. Robin.

Priscilla nodded. "I have sixty large ones and sixty small ones. I hope I run out of large ones first."

Mrs. Robin smiled. "We hope so, too. Do you have money to make change?"

Priscilla patted her pocket. "I have two dollars in change. I have a shoe box to use as a bank. And to watch my bank, I have a trained guard dog."

"Raf-raf!" barked Pow-wow.

"Good luck!" called Mr. and Mrs. Robin.

"Sell lots of lemonade!" called Eve.

Priscilla pulled her wagon along the sidewalk. Pow-wow trotted alongside. The day was sunny and already warm. In an hour it would be hot. "This is a perfect lemonade-stand day," said Priscilla. "That quiet, shady spot at the top of the hill is a perfect lemonade-stand spot."

Pow-wow saw the sign before Priscilla did.
"Raf-raf!"
It was tacked to a maple tree on Half-Mile Hill Road. It said:

Priscilla's stomach got knotty. Her palms began to sweat. She stopped her wagon to read the sign a second time. She turned to Pow-wow. "Do you think Eve put up that sign? Early this morning? As a surprise?"

"Wrrrrrouuu," howled Pow-wow.

Priscilla's stomach knotted up some more. She

wiped her sweaty palms on her shorts and took hold of the wagon handle. "If Eve didn't do it, we'd better see who did."

The next sign was taped to a telephone pole.

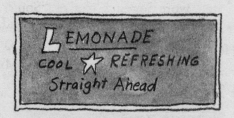

After that there were signs taped to every lamppost, telephone pole, and mailbox.

Priscilla walked faster. She trotted. She ran. The wagonful of lemonade rumbled behind her.

"*Raf-raf.*" Pow-wow ran alongside.

They rounded the last curve on Half-Mile Hill Road. Pow-wow stopped. Priscilla stopped. The wagon banged into the back of her knees.

Straight ahead stood a crowd of people. Some held bikes. Some wore jogging clothes. Some pushed baby carriages or strollers. They all looked hot. They all looked thirsty. They all were lined up facing the quiet, shady spot at the top of the hill. The sign on the shade tree said:

FELICITY'S HILLTOP LEMONADE

A long table stood underneath the tree. The cloth that covered it was pink and yellow with ruffles. On top of the cloth sat six pitchers of lemonade. Three, pale yellow. Three, bright pink. The sign on the table said:

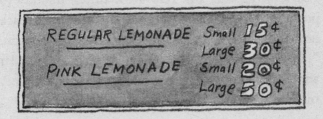

```
REGULAR LEMONADE   Small  15¢
                   Large  30¢
PINK LEMONADE      Small  20¢
                   Large  50¢
```

Behind the table stood Felicity. Her ruffled sunsuit matched the tablecloth. A fat yellow bangle bracelet clattered against a fat pink one as she poured glass after glass of lemonade.

Priscilla watched a boy pay Felicity for a regular lemonade, *large*. He said, "This stand is a great idea. You'll make lots of money."

Felicity said, "That's true, and I deserve every penny. A person should be rewarded when she has a good idea."

"Rrrrrggggh," growled Pow-wow.

What a snake! thought Priscilla. Aloud, so that Felicity would hear, she said, *"Ahhhh-hemm!"*

Felicity looked. For a moment she stopped pouring. Then she said, "If you're waiting for lemonade, little girl, the line starts back there."

It took Priscilla and Pow-wow fifteen minutes to pull the wagonful of cups, ice, and lemonade back home. It took Priscilla fifteen seconds to explain, "Her stand is fancy. Her lemonade comes in regular and pink. She stole my spot. She's getting all my money!"

"What a shame," said Mrs. Robin.

"Tough break." Mr. Robin patted Priscilla's shoulder.

Eve stroked the air with her tennis racket. "You shouldn't have told her your plan. That Felicity would steal the ears off a dog."

"Wrouuuuuuuu," whined Pow-wow.

"Don't give up," said Mrs. Robin. "Find another spot."

"There is no other spot," sniffled Priscilla. "No spot that's good."

"D.J. and I are going to play tennis in the park. Why not come and set up your stand there?" said Eve.

"There are thirsty softball players and skateboarders in the park," said Mr. Robin.

"There are thirsty rope jumpers and children on the jungle gyms," said Mrs. Robin.

Priscilla said, "There are also ice-cream trucks, soda machines, and water fountains."

"Lemonade is more fun than water," said Mrs. Robin.

"Lemonade is more refreshing than soda. It's

healthier than ice cream," said Mr. Robin.

Eve swung her racket. "Besides, people think a little kid with a lemonade stand is sort of cute. They'll buy your stuff even if it's watery and warm."

"My lemonade is the best!" said Priscilla.

"That's what you can call your stand," said Mr. Robin. "Priscilla's Best Lemonade."

"Give it a try," said Mrs. Robin.

"What have you got to lose?" said Eve.

"*Raf-raf,*" yipped Pow-wow.

Priscilla stared at her wagon. "Wel-ll . . ."

That Saturday Priscilla earned $6.35. "I would have made more if I had gotten here earlier," she told Mr. Robin when he came to help her home at five o'clock. She felt proud. She felt rich.

Mr. Robin said, "I'm pretty thirsty. I'll take a large glass before you close." He handed Priscilla a quarter. He carried his cup over to the baseball diamond to watch the end of a game.

Priscilla began stacking cups and putting the tops on her lemonade jars. If she got to the park by nine-thirty on Sunday morning, she could sell lots more. She could—

"You call this setup a lemonade stand?"

"Rrrrrggggggh," growled Pow-wow.

Priscilla knew before she looked, who was speaking with that nasty voice.

Felicity stood with her feet planted on either side of the biggest, pinkest bike in town. It had horns, lights, mirrors, and reflectors. Streamers hung from the handlebars. The bike was so big that the wheels came up to the pink and yellow ruffles on Felicity's chest. The seat came up to the ruffles on her shoulders. The handlebars were level with her nose. Felicity couldn't sit when she rode around town. She wasn't tall enough to reach both the pedals and the seat. "I closed my stand hours ago," she said. "I had to. I had no lemonade left."

"Congratulations," said Priscilla. She took down her sign.

"How much money did you make? I made seventeen dollars and fifteen cents."

Priscilla didn't want to say.

"Well?" said Felicity. "How much? Twenty dollars. Fifteen dollars?"

"I made almost seven dollars," said Priscilla.

Felicity said, "Seven dollars! Is that all?"

"I might earn more tomorrow," said Priscilla.

Felicity shook her head. "Not a chance. The only one who will earn more money is me!" She climbed on the big pink bicycle and rode shakily away.

"Wrrrrouuuuu," howled Pow-wow.

Mr. Robin returned from the baseball diamond. "All set to leave?"

"I guess so." Priscilla kicked a wheel of the wagon. She didn't feel proud. She didn't feel rich. She kicked the wagon wheel again. "Felicity Doll is a snake and a thief."

On Sunday lots of people came to the park. Most of them brought coolers, and those coolers were filled with cold drinks. At the end of the day Priscilla had made only $5.55. She pulled her wagon over the sidewalk toward home. Pow-wow trotted alongside.

Behhh-behhh! tooted a bike horn. Felicity rode up

on her big pink bike. She coasted next to Priscilla. "You've got lots of lemonade left. I'll bet you made hardly any money today."

Priscilla kept walking. "Maybe I did. Maybe I didn't."

Felicity said, "I made twenty-one dollars—"

"Twenty-one!" Priscilla stopped. "You sold more lemonade than yesterday?"

"I sold less," said Felicity. "But I charged more. I raised all my prices by fifty cents."

"Rrrrgggh," growled Pow-wow.

"People won't pay that much." Priscilla started walking again.

"They will if they're hot and thirsty." Felicity smiled her snaky smile. "Not only that, I charged for water and ice cubes. Twenty-five cents each. People complained, but they paid. They didn't have any choice."

Felicity's ruffles fluttered as she rode shakily away.

"Felicity is charging for water?" said Mrs. Robin at dinner that night.

Mr. Robin served himself some potato salad. "Charging extra for ice doesn't seem right."

Priscilla slumped back in her seat. "People are thirsty when they get to the top of the hill. There's no place else for them to get a drink. Felicity can charge as much as she likes."

"Rrrrgggggh," growled Pow-wow under the table. Eve said, "What a snake."

On Monday Felicity wore a T-shirt to school that looked just like her tablecloth. It was yellow and pink. It had a big fat ruffle around the bottom. Across the chest it said:

FELICITY'S HILLTOP LEMONADE

During Show-and-Tell Felicity bragged about how much money she'd made. She said, "Priscilla had a lemonade stand, too. Hers was a failure. She made chicken feed compared with me."

Ms. Tweet said, "You chose the perfect spot for your lemonade stand. Priscilla wasn't as lucky."

Priscilla shot up her hand. "Felicity stole that spot—"

"Show-and-Tell is over, Priscilla," said Ms. Tweet. "Let's all take out our math workbooks."

"Hey, Priscilla," hissed Felicity. "Next weekend I'm raising my prices even more!"

The following Saturday Priscilla got up very early. She was going to try a new spot. She was going to set up her stand outside the town library. She went to the kitchen and mixed six batches of lemonade. She put the cooler in her wagon and filled it with ice. On the side of the wagon she hung her sign:

Priscilla's BEST Lemonade
small 10¢ large 25¢

She and Pow-wow started down the street.

"Wouldn't it be shorter to go by way of Half-Mile Hill Road?" called Mrs. Robin.

"Arrrrrouuuuuu," yowled Pow-wow.

Priscilla shouted, "This way is longer, but this

way we don't have to pass Felicity's Hilltop
Lemonade."

That morning Priscilla sold twenty-seven cups of
lemonade. She made lots of money, but she had forgotten one thing. On Saturdays the library closed at
one o'clock. Once it closed, there were no more people to buy cold drinks.

Priscilla's stomach rumbled. She hadn't brought a
sandwich for lunch. She couldn't think of another
spot to set up her stand. The sun was hot. She was
very warm and very hungry. So was Pow-wow.

Priscilla packed her wagon. "Let's go home," she
said.

Pow-wow started back the way they had come.

"I'm too tired to go the long way," said Priscilla.
"Half-Mile Hill Road is shorter. Felicity won't see
us. The crowd at her lemonade stand will be in the
way."

Half-Mile Hill was hard to go up on a bike. It was
harder to go up on foot with a wagonful of

lemonade. By the time she was halfway up, Priscilla was out of breath. Pow-wow was panting. By the time she reached Felicity's house, Priscilla's arms ached from pulling. Pow-wow's tongue was hanging out. By the time she reached the top of the hill, Priscilla didn't care whether or not Felicity saw them. She stopped the wagon and said to Pow-wow, "You need a drink, and so do I." She poured water for Pow-wow. She poured lemonade for herself. While they drank, they looked at the crowd across the street.

Some people had bikes. Some wore jogging clothes. Some pushed strollers or baby carriages. But instead of smiling as the people the first weekend had, these people frowned. They grumbled. Priscilla looked at Felicity's sign and saw why.

FELICITY'S HILLTOP LEMONADE
Extra-Fancy Pink large $2.00
Small $1.75
Water $.75 with ice add $.50

"Look, another lemonade stand!"

Priscilla looked. A jogger had turned away from Felicity's stand. He was pointing straight at Priscilla's wagon.

A bike rider yelled, "That girl's prices are more reasonable. I'm buying from her!"

"Me, too," cried the jogger.

"So am I," shouted someone else.

People ran from Felicity's stand. They crossed the street to crowd around Priscilla's wagon.

"I'll take one large."

"Two smalls, please."

"I need one large and one small."

"Hey!" Felicity burst through the crowd. "This is private lemonade-stand territory. You're trespassing, Priscilla!"

"This is a free country," said the bike rider.

The jogger nodded. "This girl can sell lemonade anywhere she wants."

"She's a copycat! Everyone knows I was here first. Besides"—Felicity fluffed her pink and yellow ruffles—"my lemonade is better than hers."

"Is yours fresh or frozen?" said a man with a stroller.

"Frozen," said Felicity.

"Fresh," said Priscilla. "Mine is fresh!"

"Chilled or warm?" said a roller skater.

"Warm," said Felicity. "But for fifty cents you can have an ice cube."

Priscilla said, "Mine's chilled, and ice is included."

The jogger turned to Felicity. "Your lemonade isn't fresh. It isn't chilled. What makes it better?"

"Look for yourself," said Felicity crossly. "It's pink!"

"Chilled is more refreshing," said the bike rider.

"Fresh is healthier," said the man with the stroller.

The roller skater said, "That fancy lemonade stand has gotten too expensive. I'd rather have fresh cold lemonade with no frills!"

She bought a large lemonade from Priscilla. So did the bike rider. So did the man with the stroller. Felicity had no customers left.

◻   ◻   ◻

"I sold every drop and earned fourteen dollars and thirty cents," said Priscilla at dinner that night.

"What happened to Felicity?" Mr. Robin helped himself to beets.

Priscilla took a piece of garlic bread. "Felicity closed her stand for good. She went inside and watched TV."

"Her prices were too high," said Eve.

Mr. Robin said, "Priscilla put her out of business with good value and no frills."

Eve said, "That's a good name, Priscilla's No-Frills Lemonade."

"I like, Priscilla's Best," said Priscilla. She dropped half her garlic bread, not exactly by accident.

"Raf-raf!" Pow-wow snatched it up.

Priscilla ate the other half. "Besides, if I were going to change the name of my stand, I wouldn't call it No-Frills. A better name—a much better name would be Priscilla's No-Ruffles."

2 | My Weekend

*B*rrrrrnnnnnnnggg rang the school bell on Monday morning.

Behind Ms. Tweet's desk sat a substitute. Ms. Alfresco was very tall, very energetic, and very young.

"She looks like somebody's big sister," whispered Felicity to Priscilla.

Instead of driving to school in a car, Ms. Alfresco

had coasted up on a tall, shiny black bike. Instead of staying seated at her desk, she paced up and down the classroom. Instead of giving the children long, hard looks, she smiled a lot.

Twice before roll call, Anthony said he had to go to the restroom.

Ms. Alfresco believed him.

Roger said he'd done his homework but left it home.

"Me, too," said Erin.

Ms. Alfresco believed them.

"This substitute will believe anything," whispered Felicity to Priscilla.

Priscilla nodded. Her hands began to sweat, and she felt nervous.

After Ms. Alfresco collected homework, she made announcements. She told the class they would begin each school day with stretching exercises. Every day after lunch they would take a brisk nature walk.

Priscilla didn't mind exercises. She liked the idea of nature walks. She admired Ms. Alfresco's tall, shiny black bike. She had only one serious worry about smiley, energetic Ms. Alfresco. Would she know how to handle Felicity?

After announcements Ms. Alfresco said, "This morning each of us will tell how we spent the weekend."

Roger raised his hand. "We do Show-and-Tell on Monday mornings."

"We never do My Weekend," said Maggie.

Butch said, "I brought my model rocket to show. Ms. Tweet said—"

"Settle down, class." Ms. Alfresco's voice was cheerful. "Show-and-Tell is a fine activity. But while I am your teacher, we will do My Weekend. Questions?"

Butch raised his hand. "How long will Ms. Tweet be sick?"

Ms. Alfresco said, "She needs lots of bed rest. She'll stay home for three or four weeks."

Butch sighed. He stuffed the rocket back inside his desk.

Erin raised her hand. "I do boring things on the

weekend. When it's my turn, what will I say?"

"Me, too," said Roger.

"I never do anything interesting," said Gloria.

Felicity raised her hand. "I think Show-and-Tell is boring. My Weekend is a much better activity."

"Thank you, Felicity."

"If people know they have to tell about their weekends, they'll try hard to do something interesting."

Ms. Alfresco beamed. "Very good, Felicity! That's my feeling, too." She turned to write on the blackboard, "My Weekend." She used colored chalks to draw flowers on either side of it and a smiley face underneath.

"Hey, Priscilla," hissed Felicity. She settled back in her chair, "Guess who's going to be Ms. Alfresco's pet?"

"To begin," said Ms. Alfresco, "I'll tell about my weekend. I took a bicycle trip with three friends. On Saturday we rode to Broken Rock Park. We cooked dinner over a fire, and we camped out. I saw two shooting stars and heard ten sorts of songbirds. On

Sunday we rode home." She smiled. "Who would like to go next?"

"Me!Me!Me!" Felicity waved her hand.

Ms. Alfresco nodded. "Stand and tell us."

Felicity stood. She fluffed the ruffles of her orange plaid dress. She smiled a snaky smile right at Priscilla, and then she turned to the class. "On Saturday morning I went to work at my fancy lemonade stand, but Priscilla Robin copied. She started selling cheap lemonade across the street—"

"I did not copy!" cried Priscilla.

Ms. Alfresco clapped. "Girls! Girls!" When things quieted down, she said, "Go on, Felicity."

Felicity gave her ruffles another fluff. "Priscilla stole my customers, so I went inside and watched 'Dance Party.' I have my own color TV—"

"But that's terrible," said Ms. Alfresco.

Felicity nodded. "Priscilla should be punished for what she did to me."

"I'm not talking about what Priscilla did. Competition is healthy," said Ms. Alfresco. "I'm talking about wasting your Saturday in front of TV. How did you spend the rest of that beautiful afternoon?"

Felicity hung her head. "I watched 'Becky and Biff, On the Go!'"

"More television?" Ms. Alfresco looked shocked.

Erin said, "I've seen that program. It's about a sister and brother. They go all over the place, having adventures and doing good deeds."

Ms. Alfresco cheered up. "That's the idea. You children can have adventures, too. You can do your own good deeds." She turned to Felicity. "Next Monday we'll look forward to a livelier report. No more Saturday-afternoon TV."

On Friday afternoon the final bell rang *Brrrrrnnnnggggg*.

"Everyone have an active exciting weekend," urged Ms. Alfresco. "Class dismissed."

Priscilla collected her books. She put on her sweater. She hurried out of the classroom. Felicity was waiting for her on the school front steps. She fluffed her ruffles. "I'm going to have big adventures this weekend."

"Like what?" said Priscilla.

"You'll hear about them on Monday." Felicity gave Priscilla an unfriendly nudge. "What boring thing are you going to do?"

"Wel-ll . . ." Priscilla didn't want to say, but when Felicity gave her that hard look, she didn't feel as though she had a choice. "On Saturday I'm going to run my lemonade stand—"

"Borrrrringg," said Felicity. "What about Sunday?"

"On Sunday I'll make a get-well card for Ms. Tweet. I'll ride my bike to her house and put it in her mailbox. I might have an adventure on the way."

"Those are about the dullest plans I've ever heard," said Felicity.

"Who cares what you think?" Priscilla gripped her schoolbooks more tightly. She hurried past Felicity. She found her bike in the bike racks. She dumped her books in the basket. The trouble was, her weekend plans did sound dull. Priscilla wondered what those big adventures of Felicity's would be.

❑   ❑   ❑

On Monday morning Priscilla didn't want to give her My Weekend report. She scrunched down in her chair. Ms. Alfresco smiled at her anyway. "Priscilla, let's hear from you."

Slowly Priscilla stood. She twisted a corner of her sweater. "On Saturday I sold lemonade. I didn't sell much because the weather was cool. But I did give ice to a man who had hurt his ankle running. On Sunday I made a get-well card for Ms. Tweet. I was going to—"

"No *I—was—going—to's*," said Ms. Alfresco. She said it in a nice way, but Priscilla felt her face get hot just the same. "*I-was-going-to's* don't count. Let's hear what you did do."

"On Sunday it rained. I mailed my card to Ms. Tweet, and then my father and I cleaned our garage." Priscilla felt her face get even hotter. Cleaning out the garage was just about the most boring thing anyone could do.

Ms. Alfresco smiled. "That's fine, Priscilla. Butch, will you go next?"

Butch stood. "I have this model rocket—"

"You have *a* model rocket," corrected Ms. Alfresco.

Butch went on. "On Saturday I took it to the park. . . ."

"Hey, Priscilla," hissed Felicity.

Priscilla didn't look.

"Hey, Priscilla."

This time Priscilla looked.

"Here's what I think of your weekend." Felicity opened her mouth in a giant yawn.

"Felicity, are you finding your classmates' reports tiresome?"

Felicity started. She looked around the classroom. Butch had finished his report, and Ms. Alfresco was staring right at her.

Priscilla held her breath. The rest of the class held theirs. Felicity could get into big trouble—

Felicity sat up very straight. "I'm finding my classmates' reports thrilling. Especially the part in Priscilla's about cleaning the garage."

"*Hmmmmm.*" Ms. Alfresco didn't sound convinced.

Felicity said, "I yawned only because I'm tired from my own active, exciting weekend."

Ms. Alfresco nodded, "We're curious to hear what you did."

Felicity gave her ruffles a fluff and stood. "First, my parents decided we would go on a canoe trip. We paddled up a river to where it was woodsy. We cooked out. We climbed into sleeping bags and went to sleep. Then somebody yelled. It was my father. A fierce wolf was ready to attack him. My mother fainted. My big sister, Nanette, started to cry. I threw my shoe, and the wolf ran. I guess I saved my father's life."

"My word!" said Ms. Alfresco. "I had no idea there were wolves in this area. How fortunate your family was to see one."

"There's more," said Felicity. "On the way home we stopped at a hospital. I visited lots of sick children and cheered them up."

"Excellent!" said Ms. Alfresco. "Class, you may use Felicity as your example. She knows how to get the most out of a weekend."

Felicity looked at her desk and pretended to be embarrassed. Ms. Alfresco turned to lower the window shade. Felicity stopped looking embarrassed. She turned to Priscilla and stuck out her tongue.

After school that day everyone crowded around Felicity.

Roger said, "I wish my parents would take me canoeing."

Anthony said, "How big was the wolf? How big were his teeth?"

Erin said, "At the hospital did you see lots of blood?"

"I saw your parents on Saturday afternoon," said Priscilla. "They drove past my lemonade stand. They didn't have a canoe. They had a car full of golf clubs."

"We went canoeing later," said Felicity.

"Oh," said Priscilla.

At dinner that night Priscilla told her family all about Felicity's weekend.

Mr. Robin said, "That's odd. Except for golfing, Dolores Doll isn't the outdoor type."

Mrs. Robin said, "Neither is DeWitt. He spends his free time shopping at the mall."

"Why did Felicity waste a shoe? Why didn't she just give that wolf a snakebite?" Eve started to laugh.

"Arrowwww," yowled Pow-wow under the table.

"That's enough, Eve," said Mrs. Robin.

Mr. Robin said, "It does sound as though the Dolls had an exciting weekend."

"My next weekend is going to be exciting, too," said Priscilla.

"What about your lemonade stand?" said Mrs. Robin.

"I'll sell lemonade on Saturday. On Sunday Pow-wow and I will take my kite to the park. I'm going to fly it higher than anybody has ever flown one. Then, as a good deed, I'll let some little kids fly it, too."

"That's a good plan," said Mr. Robin.

Eve said, "What if one of those little kids lets go? You'll lose your kite."

Priscilla shrugged. "If I lose it, that will be a sort of adventure."

□   □   □

Saturday's weather was windy and cold.

Sunday's weather was warm with no wind.

On Monday morning Ms. Alfresco said, "Who'll tell first about his or her weekend?"

Priscilla thought she had better get her report over with as quickly as she could. She raised her hand and stood. "On Saturday I sold lemonade, but no customers came because the weather was cold and windy. On Sunday my dog and I tried to fly my kite, but it wouldn't fly because there wasn't any wind." She sat.

"You had some bad luck," said Ms. Alfresco. "Saturday was the better kite day. Sunday, the day for lemonade." She turned to Roger. "Tell us about your weekend."

Roger stood and began to speak.

"Hey, Priscilla, here's what I think of your weekend," hissed Felicity. She held her nose, "Stink-ky—!"

"Felicity, have you something to share?" said Ms. Alfresco.

Felicity scrambled to her feet. She fluffed her ruffles.

Priscilla thought, I'll bet Felicity didn't have adventures this weekend. I'll bet she watched TV.

"On Saturday my family had a fire drill. We planned the ways we would leave our bedrooms."

"Excellent," said Ms. Alfresco. "Every family should have a plan."

"We had to climb out our windows on rope ladders."

"Oooooooo!" said everyone.

"It was scary, but I was brave," said Felicity. "On Sunday one of our rich friends took my sister and me for a ride in her private airplane. She let me try the controls."

"Ooooooooooo!" said everyone.

"Well done, Felicity. You've had another active, learning-filled weekend!" Ms. Alfresco smiled.

After school Felicity was waiting beside the bike racks for Priscilla. "Too bad you couldn't get that kite of yours to fly," she said. "Too bad you couldn't go up in a plane the way I did."

"Planes aren't so great." Priscilla dumped her

schoolbooks into her bike basket. She couldn't help admitting, "I *would* like to climb one of those rope ladders." Then she thought of something. "I was at my lemonade stand all day Saturday. I didn't see your fire drill."

Felicity looked surprised. "Did I say Saturday? I meant Sunday. We flew in the plane on *Saturday*. *Sunday* we had the fire drill."

"That explains why I didn't see it," said Priscilla. "On Sunday I was in the park."

Felicity fiddled with Priscilla's bike bell. "Too bad your family has no rich friends and no fun ideas. Weekend reports must be *so-o* embarrassing for you."

At dinner that night Priscilla grumbled, "Our family has dull weekends. We need fun ideas and rich friends. I need something interesting to report next Monday."

"Is that all?" said Mr. Robin.

Mrs. Robin smiled. "Cheer up. We have good news for both you and Eve."

Priscilla looked at Eve.

Eve looked at Priscilla.

"Next weekend you'll have overnight guests. Your cousins Chipp and Sissy are coming to stay."

"Sissy bites!" said Eve.

Priscilla said, "Chipp is bossy. He makes Pow-wow fetch and play dead."

"*Arrrrouuuuu,*" yowled Pow-wow under the table.

"That was last year," said Mrs. Robin. "You've all grown up a lot since then."

Mr. Robin said, "I'll bet Chipp and Sissy will know some exciting things for you to do."

When their guests arrived the following Saturday, Priscilla said, "We can fish in the pond. We can ride bikes to the park. We can set up my lemonade stand. We can *try* to fly kites—"

"Not today," said Sissy. "There's only one thing Chipp and I like to do on Saturday afternoons."

Chipp said, "We watch 'Becky and Biff, On the Go!'"

"TV?" said Eve. "That's boring."

Sissy shook her head. "You're wrong. Becky and Biff do neat things. Last week they had a fire drill at their house. They climbed down scary rope ladders. Later a rich friend took them for a ride in her plane."

Eve looked at Priscilla.

Priscilla said, "I'll bet Biff and Becky got to try the controls."

"That's right!" Chipp nodded. "The week before that, Biff and Becky went on a canoe trip. They camped out. A fierce wolf almost attacked Biff."

"I'll bet Becky frightened the wolf and saved Biff," said Eve.

"She threw a shoe," said Sissy.

"I'll bet Biff and Becky visited a hospital later. I'll bet they cheered up sick children," said Priscilla.

Chipp scratched his head. "Are you sure you didn't see those shows?"

Eve shook her head. "Priscilla and I never watch 'Becky and Biff.' But today I think we should."

Priscilla nodded. "You're our guests. If you want to watch, that's what we'll do."

Sissy said, "Oh, good! Today Becky and Biff are

going on a bike trip. They're going to stumble into the camp of some poor but honest gypsies."

"What channel?" said Eve.

"Who wants to be first to report on her weekend?" Ms. Alfresco looked at Priscilla.

Priscilla shook her head. "Today I'd rather not go first."

"I'll go first," said Butch.

"Very well," said Ms. Alfresco.

Butch stood. "On Saturday I learned how to do a wheelie on my skateboard. That's how I got this." He pushed up his sleeve and showed the class his scraped arm. "Sunday I caught bugs for my frog to eat."

"Congratulations," said Ms. Alfresco. "The wheelie is a hard move to learn. Who would like to go next? Gloria?"

Gloria stood. "On Saturday my father was sick. I made honey toast for him and crackers with peanut butter. He didn't eat them, so I did. On Sunday my cat climbed a tree. I rescued him."

"I hope your father is feeling better," said Ms. Alfresco. "Felicity, would you like to go next?"

"Priscilla should go before me," said Felicity. "Her weekends are dull. Mine are exciting. If she goes after me, hers will sound even more boring than usual."

Ms. Alfresco turned to Priscilla. "It's true that Felicity's weekends are hard to top."

"I don't mind," said Priscilla. "I'd rather go after her."

"Very well," said Ms. Alfresco.

"You'll be sorry, Priscilla!" hissed Felicity. She stood. In her normal voice she said, "On Saturday my parents and I went on a bike trip."

"Excellent!" said Ms. Alfresco. "There's nothing like a trip on a bike."

"We rode over hills and through woods. We came to a place we had never before seen. We were lost."

"Ooooooooo," said everyone.

"Then we stumbled into the camp of some poor but honest gypsies."

"How unusual!" said Ms. Alfresco.

Felicity said, "The gypsies shared their food with

us. They played guitars and told my fortune. They said I'll have good luck all my life."

"You certainly had good luck meeting them," said Ms. Alfresco. She turned. "Now, Priscilla, let's hear from you."

Priscilla stood. She pretended not to see the nasty look Felicity gave her. She said, "My cousins came for the weekend. They were guests, so we had to do what they wanted. What they wanted to do was watch TV."

"TV?" said Ms. Alfresco. "I hope you didn't agree?"

Priscilla shrugged. "I said we could go fishing, or fly kites, or sell lemonade."

"Those were all fine suggestions. What did your cousins say?"

"They said we should watch TV, instead. Their favorite program was on, 'Becky and Biff, On the Go!'"

"Isn't that the program you once watched?" said Ms. Alfresco to Felicity. "Before you started having active exciting weekends?"

Felicity looked from Priscilla to Ms. Alfresco. "It *miiiight* have been."

Priscilla said, "I didn't think I'd like that program, but it was sort of interesting. First—"

"Nobody wants to hear about a TV program," said Felicity. "You're supposed to tell about your weekend!"

"Priscilla has the floor." Ms. Alfresco smiled. "Let's give her our attention."

Priscilla said, "Becky and Biff went on a bike trip. They stumbled into the camp of some poor but honest gypsies."

"More gypsies?" said Ms. Alfresco.

"The gypsies shared their food and played guitars and told Becky's and Biff's fortunes."

Ms. Alfresco frowned at Felicity. "Go on, Priscilla."

"It was a good program," said Priscilla. "But my cousins said that last week was even better. Last week Becky and Biff had a fire drill at their house. Later a rich friend took them up in her airplane. And the week before that they took a canoe trip, and

Becky saved Biff from a fierce wolf—"

"Thank you, Priscilla. That will be all." Ms. Alfresco was looking hard at Felicity.

"I haven't told what I did on Sunday," said Priscilla.

Ms. Alfresco repeated, "That will be all."

Priscilla sat.

After school Felicity was waiting beside the bike racks for Priscilla. "Thanks for getting me into trouble," she said.

Priscilla dumped her books into her bike basket. "Don't blame me. I only told what I did on the weekend."

"Ms. Alfresco is making me take home a note to my parents." Felicity showed Priscilla the envelope inside her notebook.

"Too bad," said Priscilla. She pointed to a second envelope. "What's that?"

Felicity snapped shut the notebook. "That's a card I made for Ms. Tweet. I told her to get well soon. I'm tired of being Ms. Alfresco's pet."

3 | Study Buddies

That Friday, when Priscilla brought home the first terrible spelling test, Mrs. Robin said, "Don't worry. You just had a bad day."

The following Friday, when she brought home the second test, Mr. Robin said, "You're not the first person to misspell *recipe* and *further*. When I was your age . . ."

The next Friday, when Priscilla brought home the

third spelling test with a big red D on top, Mr. Robin frowned.

Mrs. Robin shook her head.

"Look how she spelled *yacht*," said Eve. "Y–a–h–t–e!"

"I spelled it right at first," said Priscilla. "But it looked funny, so I changed it."

"You changed *settle*, too," said Eve. "I can see the eraser mark. You've got it spelled s-e-t-t-e-l. Priscilla deserves A for originality."

"*Arrrouuu,*" whined Pow-wow under the table.

"It's not funny," said Priscilla. "If I get one more bad mark on a spelling test, I'll have to have a study buddy."

"Study buddy?" said Mrs. Robin.

Mr. Robin said, "What's that?"

"S-t-u-d-y B-u-d-d-y," spelled Eve. "A study buddy is someone who's good at a subject. If you're a study buddy, you help a classmate who's having trouble with the subject you're good at. If Priscilla needs a study buddy for spelling, Ms. Tweet will give her the best speller in the class. They'll work together for half an hour each day until Priscilla's grades improve."

"That sounds like an excellent program," said Mr. Robin.

Eve nodded. "Some study buddies get along so well they turn into best friends."

"You don't say?" Mrs. Robin cocked her head. She turned to Priscilla. "This study buddy plan sounds ideal. If I were you, I'd look forward to getting help from the best speller in the class."

"*Wrrrrouuuu,*" yowled Pow-wow.

Priscilla shook her head. "That's about the worst thing that could happen to me."

Eve said, "Unh-oh, I think I know who that best speller must be."

"Oh, dear," said Mrs. Robin.

"My, my." Mr. Robin looked concerned.

Priscilla nodded. "She gets a hundred on every test. The best speller is Felicity."

"*Arrrrouuuu,*" yowled Pow-wow.

Everyone looked grim.

After a minute Eve brightened. "Felicity wouldn't

do anything to help anyone, ever. Ms. Tweet may ask her to be Priscilla's study buddy, but Felicity will definitely say no."

"Eve is right," said Mrs. Robin.

"I never thought of that," said Priscilla.

Mr. Robin nodded slowly. "Just to be on the safe side, Priscilla had better study extra-hard this week."

All week long Priscilla studied the new spelling words. Eve helped her.

"Bakeries," read Eve from the list.

Priscilla thought a minute. She stared at the ceiling. "B-a-k-e-r-i-e-s."

"Good," said Eve. *"Chief."*

Friday came. Priscilla felt jittery. She also felt ready for the test. She hurried into school and found Felicity waiting beside her desk.

"I'll bet you're nervous." Felicity smiled one of her snaky smiles.

Priscilla put down her pencil case. She put down her spelling book. She put down her lunch box. "I don't know what you mean." Her hands shook. She hoped Felicity didn't notice. "I feel perfectly fine."

"Ha! You can't fool me," said Felicity. "This morning we have a spelling test. You're the worst speller in the c-l-a-s-s. One more bad mark, and you'll probably have to stay b-a-c-k. If I were you, I would be shaking in my ugly s-h-o-e-s!"

Brnnnnggggggg rang the bell.

"Take your seats, class. We have lots to do this morning," said Ms. Tweet. She handed out paper for the spelling test. "Write your name at the top and number from one to twenty."

Anthony and Erin numbered. So did Roger. So did Felicity. Priscilla numbered, too.

"Let's begin," said Ms. Tweet. "*Bakeries*. There are four *bakeries* on Water Street. *Bakeries*."

Anthony bent over his paper and wrote. So did Erin, Roger, and Felicity. Priscilla wrote, too. "B-a-k-e-r-i-e-s." She lifted her pencil and looked at what she had written. The word looked funny. She thought, I put in one *e* too many. She erased and tried again. "B-a-k-r-i-e-s." That looked better.

"Chief," said Ms. Tweet. "The president is our commander in chief."

When the test was over, everyone exchanged papers. Priscilla exchanged with Erin. Ms. Tweet called on different children to spell aloud each word. Everyone listened and corrected the papers. When corrections were done, everyone passed the papers back.

"I'm sorry," said Erin to Priscilla.

Priscilla looked at her test. Word after word had a red X beside it. At the top of the page was the grade, "55. E."

"Hey, Priscilla," hissed Felicity from across the aisle. "Look what I got!" She held up her test.

"100," said the grade. "A + ."

Felicity smiled a snaky smile. "How did you do?"

"No chatting, class. Everyone pass his or her test forward."

Priscilla took the tests that Anthony passed forward. She stuffed hers in the middle where no one would see the big red E. She passed the pile ahead.

When the papers reached the front, Ms. Tweet collected them. She gave each one a quick glance. "Erin, you made a careless mistake on *matches*."

"I left out the *t*," said Erin. "But I still got a ninety."

"Roger, what is the rule that applies to *receive*?"

"'*I* before *e*, except after *c*,'" said Roger. "I forgot the 'except' part. Otherwise, I would have gotten an eighty-five."

"Felicity, you earned another perfect score. How many one-hundreds does this make for you?" said Ms. Tweet.

Felicity fluffed her ruffles and pretended to be embarrassed. "It makes eleven one-hundreds. I guess I'm some kind of spelling genius."

"It certainly seems that way." Ms. Tweet stared at the next test paper. "What's this, Priscilla? Fifty-five?"

Priscilla scrunched down in her chair.

"E?" said Ms. Tweet.

Anthony snickered. Maggie giggled.

Priscilla scrunched farther.

Ms. Tweet gave Anthony and Maggie a stern

look. "Priscilla is having a difficult time with spelling. Instead of laughing, let's think. How can we help her?"

Anthony raised his hand. "Give her a study buddy?"

"Exactly," said Ms. Tweet. She turned to Felicity. "You're the best speller in class. Will you help Priscilla?"

"Wel-ll . . ." Felicity twisted one of her crinkly yellow ruffles. "Priscilla's a terrible speller. Helping her would be hard work." She thought a minute. "Would she have to do as I say?"

"Priscilla doesn't want to fail spelling. She'd follow your suggestions," said Ms. Tweet.

Felicity smiled a snaky smile. "I'm too kind a person to say no. I'll be Priscilla's study buddy if she wants."

"I don't want!" said Priscilla.

"Girls!" Ms. Tweet looked stern. "I want to see you cooperate."

"But—" said Priscilla.

"On Monday you can begin work together. Now, class, let's take out our reading books."

Priscilla slumped back in her seat.

"Hey, Priscilla—" hissed Felicity from across the aisle. "This is what I'm going to do to you." She pointed to a spot on her desktop. She put her thumb on the spot and made a hard, grinding motion. Then she covered her mouth and silently laughed.

That night at dinner Priscilla said, "She's going to squash me like a bug! Tell Ms. Tweet not to make us study buddies. Please!"

"There, there," said Mr. Robin. "Let's have a look at this latest test."

Priscilla pulled the folded test out of her pocket. She handed it to Mr. Robin.

"Good heavens," he said. "This is the worst yet!"

Mrs. Robin looked. "You couldn't have studied and done this badly."

"Priscilla did study. I helped, so I know," said Eve. "Please pass me that test."

Mr. Robin passed it.

Eve looked. "You misspelled *bakeries*. You misspelled *pleasant* and *stereo*—"

"How could you misspell *stereo*?" said Mrs. Robin.

Priscilla shrugged. "It looked funny, so I put in an extra *r*."

"We worked on all these words," said Eve. "When you spelled them for me last night, you missed only one."

"I know," said Priscilla. She turned to Mr. Robin. "I'll do better next week. I promise. Just tell Ms. Tweet not to make me be study buddies with Felicity."

"Wel-ll . . ." said Mr. Robin.

Mrs. Robin said, "We didn't realize just how poorly you were doing."

"But—" said Priscilla.

"Felicity may not be your closest friend, but she is an excellent speller," said Mr. Robin.

Mrs. Robin said, "Having her as a study buddy may give you the boost you need to break out of this spelling slump."

"But—" said Priscilla.

"It can't hurt to give this study buddy business a try. Just for a few weeks," said Mr. Robin.

Mrs. Robin said, "Felicity isn't *that* bad. She's a classmate, not a—not a—"

"Snake?" suggested Eve.

Mrs. Robin frowned. "That's not what I was going to say."

On Monday morning Priscilla and Felicity sat at the long table at the back of the classroom. To one side sat math study buddies Maggie and Erin. To the other side sat reading study buddies Roger and Butch.

"I won't do it!" whispered Priscilla.

"Yes, you will," hissed Felicity. "I'm your study buddy. You have to do as I say."

"Whispers only, study buddies," said Ms. Tweet from her desk at the front of the room. "Everyone else, silent studying."

Felicity hissed, "Do it, or I'll tell Ms. Tweet you aren't cooperating."

Priscilla opened her notebook to a blank page. She opened her spelling book to the new lesson. She gripped her pencil and grumbled, "Very well. *Your wish is my command. . . .*"

Felicity frowned. "You left out the best part. Say the whole thing!"

Priscilla gripped her pencil harder. *"Your wish is my command—Your Majesty."*

Felicity fluffed her ruffles. "That's better. Copy those words, slave."

On Friday Ms. Tweet gave another spelling test. Priscilla got another 55.

"Whistle, beach ball, wilderness—" Felicity looked at Priscilla's test paper. "You knew how to spell those words. You got them wrong on purpose!"

"Why would I do that?" asked Priscilla.

Felicity frowned. "You would do it to make me, your study buddy, look bad. That's why."

"I did my best," said Priscilla. "At first I spelled them right, but then I changed them. They started to look funny."

"There's nothing funny about a study buddy of mine getting an E," said Felicity. "Next week I'll be more strict with you."

□ □ □

The following Monday Felicity handed Priscilla a piece of oaktag on a yarn loop. "Hang that around your neck," she said.

Priscilla took the oaktag from Felicity. "What is it?" After one look she shoved it back. "If you think I'll wear this, you're crazy!"

"Whispers only, study buddies," said Ms. Tweet.

"I give the orders here," hissed Felicity. "Wear it, or I'll tell Ms. Tweet you're not cooperating."

Priscilla frowned. Crossly she snatched up the oaktag. Angrily she slipped the yarn loop over her head. The sign dangled in front of her shirt. In black marker it said:

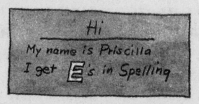

"That sign will embarrass you into spelling correctly," said Felicity. She pointed to the list of new spelling words. "Copy those. Use them in sentences.

Break them into syllables. Get to work!"

"Yes, Your Majesty." Priscilla picked up her pencil and got to work. She tried to write neatly, but her sign kept getting in the way.

On Friday Ms. Tweet gave another spelling test. Priscilla got a fifty.

"Fifty?" Ms. Tweet looked at Priscilla's test paper. She turned to Felicity. "You've tried hard, but Priscilla's spelling problem is too big for a study buddy to handle."

"Thank goodness," muttered Priscilla.

"We'll have to try something else."

Felicity clutched Ms. Tweet's sleeve. "Let me try once more, pleeeeeeeeeeeze? I have a secret plan. I promise that Priscilla will spell better next week."

"Wel-ll . . ." said Ms. Tweet. "Since you have a plan and since you're so determined . . . All right!"

"Oh, boy!" said Felicity.

Oh, no, thought Priscilla. She wondered what Felicity's secret plan could be.

◻   ◻   ◻

After school, beside the bike racks, Felicity explained. "Next week when we have our spelling test, I'll hold my paper where you can see it. You'll copy the answers from me."

"That's cheating!" said Priscilla.

"Do it, or you'll get another E," said Felicity.

"I'm no cheater!"

Felicity shrugged. "Do you want an E? Do you want to stay back?"

Priscilla kicked the bike rack. *"No-o—"*

"No, what?"

Priscilla sighed. "No, Your Majesty."

"Then copy my paper. That's the only secret plan I've got."

All weekend long Priscilla worried about what she should do. She worried every day the following week.

"Are you feeling all right?" said Mr. Robin at dinner Thursday night.

Priscilla fiddled with her brussels sprouts. "I'm okay."

Mrs. Robin said, "Ms. Tweet is sure you'll do better on tomorrow's spelling test."

"I may do better than even Ms. Tweet expects," said Priscilla.

"Wonderful!" said Mrs. Robin.

"You sound very sure of yourself," said Mr. Robin.

Eve gave Priscilla a long, hard look. "After dinner I'd like to speak with you."

"Cheating is wrong!" said Eve. "Tell Ms. Tweet to change your seat. Sit where you can't see Felicity's paper."

"There's one thing wrong with your plan," said Priscilla. "If I don't copy, I'm going to get another E."

Eve sighed. "You spell well at home. Why can't you do it at school?"

Priscilla hung her head. "I spell most words right at first, but they start to look funny, so I erase."

"Here's *my* secret plan," said Eve. "When Felicity writes, don't copy. When you write, don't erase."

"Wel-ll . . ." Priscilla wasn't so sure.

"Names at the top of your papers. Number from one to twenty," said Ms. Tweet the next day.

Priscilla looked at Felicity.

Felicity looked at Priscilla.

Priscilla made up her mind. She raised her hand. "May I change seats?"

"Change seats?" said Ms. Tweet.

Priscilla tried to ignore Felicity's glare. She said, "If I sit at the front of the room, I can concentrate better."

"Hurry and take a seat at the crafts table," said Ms. Tweet.

Priscilla hurried to her new seat. Her back was to the class. Her face was to the blackboard. She couldn't see Felicity. She couldn't copy from Felicity's paper.

Quickly she wrote her name at the top of the page, "P-r-i-s-c-i-l-l-a." She began to number from one to twenty. She stopped. She looked back at her name. Her name looked funny.

Should it be *P-r-i-c-s—* Should there be one *l* instead of two? Priscilla's hands got clammy. Her forehead got damp. She wiped her hands on her skirt. She stared at the classroom ceiling. "P-r-i-s-c-i-l-l-a," she whispered. She looked back at what she had written. *P-r-i-s-c-i-l-l-a.* It looked funny, but it must be correct.

"*Medal,*" said Ms. Tweet. "When I won the race, I earned a *medal.*"

Priscilla quickly finished numbering. Beside "1." she wrote, "m-e-d-a-l." She lifted her pencil and looked at what she had written. The word looked funny. That *a* would look better as an *e,* she thought. She started to erase. She stopped. She stared at the classroom ceiling. "M-e-d-a-l," she whispered. She looked back at what she had written. It looked funny, but it must be correct.

Priscilla spelled twenty spelling words without once erasing. Each word looked funny. Still, she left each one as she had first written it. When the test was over, she returned to her desk.

"Get ready for another E," muttered Felicity.

"No chatting," said Ms. Tweet. "Exchange papers for corrections."

Priscilla exchanged with Erin. She crossed her fingers and kept them crossed until Erin handed back the corrected test.

"One hundred?" said Ms. Tweet. "*A plus!* Class, let's congratulate Priscilla."

"Congratulations!" said everyone. Everyone except Felicity.

Felicity shot up her hand. "People are forgetting. Priscilla got that one hundred only because of me!"

Ms. Tweet smiled. "I think we should give Priscilla *some* credit. However, you're right to remind us. Your hard work and caring helped Priscilla to earn this remarkable score."

"That's better," said Felicity. When Ms. Tweet turned to put the tests on her desk, Felicity stuck out her tongue at Priscilla. "So there!"

"By the way." Ms. Tweet turned back to Felicity. "Now that the test is over, tell us. How did you help Priscilla? What was your secret plan?"

Felicity looked at Priscilla.

Priscilla looked at Felicity.

"Wel-ll . . ." said Felicity.

Ms. Tweet said, "Priscilla, will you let us in on the secret?"

Priscilla kept her eyes on Felicity. "Wel-ll . . ."

Felicity crinkled up her forehead. She made her eyes sad as though she were begging.

Priscilla turned to Ms. Tweet. "I'll tell. Felicity promised she would stay my study buddy until I got a good mark. If it took all year, she would stay my study buddy. If it took the rest of our lives, she would stay my study buddy. If it took forever and ever, she would stay my study buddy."

Felicity looked relieved.

Ms. Tweet looked pleased. "And you were so grateful that you studied extra-hard?"

Priscilla shook her head. "I studied extra-hard because I was s-c-a-r-e-d."

4 | Bike Day

That Saturday at breakfast Priscilla asked for the hundredth time, "Please, can't I get a new bike?" Priscilla's bike was small, old, and blue. It had fat tires and a straw basket in front. It had foot brakes instead of hand brakes. The handlebars only came up to Priscilla's waist. Eve had gotten the bike when it was new. Priscilla had gotten it several years later as a hand-me-down. That bike had been all right for Priscilla at age six. But Priscilla was older now. For an older girl that bike was too small, too blue— Too babyish.

Mr. Robin kept eating his cereal. "You have a perfectly fine bicycle."

"It's old, and it's rusty," said Priscilla.

"New bikes are expensive," said Mrs. Robin. "There's nothing wrong with yours that paint and polish won't fix."

"My bike is babyish," said Priscilla. "When I ride it, people make fun of me."

"People?" Mr. Robin looked up. "Which people?"

"Rrrrgggggh," growled Pow-wow under the table.

Priscilla frowned. She concentrated on sinking banana slices with her cereal spoon.

Eve said, "I'll bet *those people* are Felicity Doll."

"Felicity rides to school on a fancy pink ten-speed," said Priscilla. "It has horns and lights and mirrors and handlebar streamers."

"I've seen that bike," said Eve. "It's flashy, but it's too big for Felicity. She has to ride standing up. I'll bet that bike is as big as Ms. Alfresco's."

"It's bigger," said Priscilla. "But it's not as nice. Buzzman's Cycle Shop has a bike just like Ms. Alfresco's. It's tall. It's black. It's grown-up. Felicity couldn't make fun of it. That's the bike I'd like."

Mr. Robin folded his newspaper. "You know better than to listen to Felicity."

Mrs. Robin put the top back on the jam jar. "Felicity has always been a bit of a tease."

"That's like calling a boa constrictor a bit of a pest," said Eve. "Felicity Doll is a real snake."

"Eve!" said Mrs. Robin.

Eve got up from the table. "D.J. and I have to practice putting tourniquets on each other's legs. It's our class project for Safety Week. Bye."

The back door slammed behind her.

"What's your Safety Week project?" Mrs. Robin asked Priscilla.

Priscilla shrugged. "We haven't decided. Our weekend homework is to think of an idea." She looked from her mother to her father. "What about my bike? My old one has soft tires. The brakes don't work well. The bell is so rusty I need two hands to make it ring."

"That's unsafe," said Mr. Robin. "After breakfast we'll go to Buzzman's Cycle Shop and get you a new bell."

"Only a bell?" said Priscilla.

Mr. Robin nodded. "Today, only a bell. Isn't Bike Inspection Day coming up soon?"

Priscilla said, "It's the last day of Safety Week. That's next Friday."

"Very well," said Mr. Robin. "We'll make a bargain. If Officer Barrett passes your bike on Inspection Day, you'll ride it for one more year. No complaints."

"Another whole year?" said Priscilla.

Mr. Robin gave her a stern look.

Priscilla kept quiet.

"If Officer Barrett says your bike needs too many repairs, we'll get you a new one."

"Oh, boy!" said Priscilla.

"Raf-raf!" barked Pow-wow.

"Remember," said Mr. Robin. "We'll get the new bike only if this one fails. Is that a bargain?"

Priscilla knew her bike was sure to fail. She nodded. "It's a bargain."

On Monday morning the sun shone brightly. Priscilla wheeled her old blue bike out of the garage and started for school.

"Raf-raf!" Pow-wow ran alongside.

The new bicycle bell sparkled in the sunlight. *Brngg-brngg!* Priscilla could ring it using just her thumb. She rounded the curve of Half-Mile Hill Road. She sped down the hill.

Wind lifted Priscilla's hair from her neck. It made her sweater fly out behind her like a cape. *Brngg-brngg!* Priscilla reached the bottom of the hill. She coasted up to the big red stop sign. She pressed backward on the pedals to put on her brakes. The bike slowed to a stop.

"Hey—!"

The voice was still far away, but it was getting closer.

"Hey, you! Priscilla Robin Redbreast!"

"Rrrrgggggh," growled Pow-wow.

There was no way Priscilla could escape. She gripped her handlebars and turned.

A giant pink bike zoomed toward Priscilla down the hill. The tiny rider stood. Wind blew her hair straight out behind her. Priscilla knew that hair was curly. Speed made the rider's dress a greenish blur. Priscilla knew that dress was covered with ruffles. The rider braked to a stop beside Priscilla. She hopped off the giant bike and didn't look tiny anymore.

In her white patent leather shoes with the bows and the flowers, in her lace-trimmed socks and her ruffled chartreuse dress, Felicity Doll looked exactly the same size as she always did. Trouble size. She pointed to Priscilla's bike. "Haven't you heard? No tricycles allowed in the street!"

"Rrrrggggh," growled Pow-wow.

"It's not a tricycle!" said Priscilla.

"Oh?" Felicity leaned closer. She studied Priscilla's bike from rusty front fender to rear reflector. At last she said, "You're right. This isn't a tricycle." She looked Priscilla right in the eye. "Kiddie cars aren't allowed either."

"It's no kiddie car! It's my bike," said Priscilla.

Felicity cocked her head. "You call that pile of rust a bike? I'll bet when we have bicycle inspection, Officer Barrett won't even pass it."

"I'll bet you're right," said Priscilla. "I hope he doesn't."

Felicity stared. "If you don't pass inspection, you won't get a new license. If you don't have a license, you can't ride to school. You'll have to walk."

"Not if I have a new bike," said Priscilla. It was a mistake to tell Felicity anything, ever. But Priscilla was tired of her making fun.

"New bike? What new bike?" said Felicity.

Priscilla used a corner of her sweater to shine the bell. "If my bike passes inspection, I have to ride it for another year. If it fails, I get a new bike—a black one with narrow tires, just like Ms. Alfresco's."

"You're making that up," said Felicity.

Priscilla shook her head and crossed her heart. "My parents promised."

"Ms. Alfresco's bike is almost as fast as mine," said Felicity.

"Ms. Alfresco's bike is faster," said Priscilla. "I'll bet my new one will be faster, too."

Felicity cocked her head. "Tell me again what you have to do to get that new bike."

"Fail inspection," said Priscilla.

"And if you pass?"

"I won't pass," said Priscilla.

"But if you do?" said Felicity.

Priscilla shrugged. "I'll be stuck with this old bike for another year."

In school that day Ms. Tweet said, "We need to choose a Safety Week project. Who thought of a good idea over the weekend?"

Priscilla didn't bother to raise her hand. She wanted to think. What she thought about was the tall, shiny black bike that would be hers as soon as the old blue bike failed inspection.

"Erin?" said Ms. Tweet.

"We could learn to walk on crutches," said Erin. "In case we ever break our legs."

Ms. Tweet wrote on the blackboard:

CRUTCHES

She turned back to the class. "Randy, have you thought of a project?"

"We could ride around in an ambulance," said Randy. "We could see all the car crashes and blood that happen when people don't follow safety rules."

"A *talk* with an ambulance crew might be valuable," said Ms. Tweet. She wrote on the board:

AMBULANCE

Then she said, "Both these ideas are about what to do *after* accidents. Does anyone have a project to help us prevent them?"

"I have an idea!" Felicity raised her hand and waved it. "It's called, Project Bike Repair. We work on our bikes. We fix them so that they're clean, shiny, and safe. On Bike Inspection Day, they all pass."

"Bravo, Felicity!" said Ms. Tweet. "That's an excellent idea."

Felicity turned to Priscilla. She smiled her snaky smile.

Ms. Tweet said, "What do you think, class? Shall we make Project Bike Repair our Safety Week project? Shall we make a perfect inspection record our goal?"

"I vote for ambulance rides," said Randy.

"Bike Repair! Bike Repair!" cried everyone else.

"Can we leave out my bike?" said Priscilla. "It's old. I don't mind if it fails—"

"If Priscilla's bike fails, it will ruin things for everyone else in class," said Felicity.

Priscilla said, "But—"

Ms. Tweet shook her head. "We want that perfect record. Everyone's bike must pass."

Priscilla slumped in her seat.

Across the aisle Felicity covered her mouth and silently laughed.

□   □   □

On Tuesday all the children in Ms. Tweet's class rode their bikes to school early. They brought rags and sponges and pails and soap. Ms. Tweet brought wrenches and pliers and screwdrivers. Everyone parked. Ms. Tweet said, "All right, let's get to work."

Erin grabbed a sponge and started to wash.

Butch grabbed a screwdriver and started to unscrew.

Gloria attached a pump to her tire and started to pump.

Priscilla picked up a clean rag. She laid it over her rusty handlebar. She moved the cloth back and forth. She moved it softly so that she wouldn't remove any rust. She moved it slowly so that it would take her all morning not to remove it.

"I see what you're up to." Felicity stomped up next to her. "You think that if you don't make any repairs, you'll fail inspection."

"I'm getting rust off my handlebars. That's a repair," said Priscilla.

"That's stalling," said Felicity. She gave her ruffles

an angry fluff. "I know how to take care of you. Ms. Tweet!" she called. "Priscilla needs help. Otherwise her bike won't be ready by Friday!"

"Go fix your own bike!" said Priscilla.

Ms. Tweet finished adjusting Roger's bike chain. She came over to where Felicity and Priscilla stood. She walked all the way around Priscilla's bike. "This bike does need a lot of work. I'll help, and I'll show you what to do. Don't worry, Priscilla. We'll have your bike ready in time to pass inspection."

"But—" said Priscilla.

Brrrrrrnnnngggg! rang the school bell.

"Time to go inside, class!" called Ms. Tweet.

Felicity covered her mouth and silently snickered.

What a snake! thought Priscilla.

That afternoon Ms. Tweet tightened Priscilla's brakes. Priscilla removed rust from the handlebars and fenders. Wednesday morning Ms. Tweet patched Priscilla's soft tire. Wednesday afternoon Priscilla attached the bike pump and pumped until the tire was firm.

Thursday morning Ms. Tweet adjusted the chain. Priscilla scrubbed the whole bike with soapy water. Thursday afternoon Ms. Tweet opened cans of blue paint and white. Very carefully she touched up the bike's fenders. Very carefully she touched up the frame. Felicity watched and gave advice. "Back there, you missed a spot."

"This bike looks as good as new," said Ms. Tweet when they had finished.

"There's no chance it will fail inspection," said Felicity.

Priscilla didn't say anything. She knew they were right.

Officer Barrett arrived at school at nine-fifteen Friday morning. Students lined up in the parking lot where he waited. "Who's first?" called Officer Barrett.

Rocky Lee wheeled his bike forward.

Officer Barrett squeezed the tires. He tested the chain. He checked the brakes. He straightened up and walked all around the bike, looking for broken

spokes or rusted fenders. He made sure the bike had a rear reflector. He made sure the bell would ring. Finally he said to Rocky, "Show me how you ride and how you signal."

Rocky climbed on his bike. Much more slowly than he usually did, he pedaled around the parking lot. Much more carefully than he usually did, he signaled. *Right turn. Left turn. Stop.*

"Very good," said Officer Barrett. "This bike passes inspection. Here's your new license. Next!"

Erin wheeled her bike into the parking lot. The rest of the line moved up. Butch, Gloria, Anthony, Priscilla . . .

"Excuse me, little girl."

Priscilla felt a tap on her shoulder.

"Tricycles will be inspected in the afternoon."

Priscilla turned. Felicity was wearing a helmet and goggles. She had reflector tape wrapped around her socks just below the lace.

Priscilla felt too discouraged to answer her back. She wheeled her bike aside. "You can go ahead if you want."

Felicity frowned. "Don't think that you can get out of this by stalling. That old bike of yours is going to pass inspection."

"I know," said Priscilla.

"You're not getting any speedy new bike," said Felicity. "I fixed that."

Priscilla nodded. "That's right. You did."

Felicity shoved the pink bike at Priscilla. "Hold this for a minute."

Priscilla held it.

Felicity gave her ruffles a brisk fluff. "As long as you understand that you're going to pass, I'll go first." She took back her bike.

"Next!" called Officer Barrett.

Felicity straightened her helmet. "This won't take long." She wheeled the giant pink bike into the center of the parking lot. Priscilla watched Officer Barrett squeeze the tires, try the brakes, ring the bell, test the chain. She watched him circle the bike, looking for broken spokes or rusted fenders. She watched Felicity get on the bike and ride standing up.

"Hold it," shouted Officer Barrett.

Felicity wavered. She braked to a stop. She lurched to the ground.

"That bike is much too big for you," said Officer Barrett. "You need to be able to ride sitting down. Until you get some blocks for those pedals, I can't pass you."

"Blocks?" said Felicity.

Erin giggled. "Blocks!"

"Blocks!" Roger snickered with Anthony.

Ms. Tweet sighed. "I've seen Felicity beside her bike. I never saw her on it."

"Blocks are for tricycles. Blocks are for babies!" said Felicity.

"Blocks are for anyone whose bike is too big for her," said Officer Barrett. "When you get those blocks, you may pick up your license. Next!"

Felicity dragged her bike away and dumped it on the ground. *Blaamm!*

Priscilla wheeled her bike into the center of the parking lot.

"Well, well." Officer Barrett pushed back his hat. "This old bike has gotten some sprucing up."

Priscilla nodded.

"I remember the first time Eve brought it to inspection. It was brand-new."

"It's as good as new now," said Ms. Tweet. "Priscilla's bike was our special repair project for Safety Week."

"You don't say?" said Officer Barrett. "Then it's sure to pass." He bent over the wheels. "These tires feel firm. The foot brakes? Excellent. No rust. No broken spokes. *Brngg-brngg!* Nice bell!"

"That bell is the only thing about this bike that's new," said Priscilla.

"New or old, this bike is in tiptop shape. Care for it well, and it'll last you many, many more years."

Felicity stopped sulking. She perked up, "Priscilla won't have to get a new bike ever. Will she, Officer Barrett?"

"Just take a spin around the parking lot and show me your hand signals. Then you'll get your new license."

Priscilla sighed. She swung her leg over the bike, sank to the seat, and pedaled.

"Hold it," shouted Officer Barrett.

Priscilla swerved. She braked. She stopped.

Officer Barrett shook his head. "You've worked so hard that I hate to tell you this." He shook his head again. "I can't pass this bike of yours. For a grown-up girl like you, it's much too small."

"Too small?" said Priscilla.

"Too *what*?" cried Felicity.

"Your knees stick out when you ride. So do your elbows. That makes for unsafe biking," said Officer Barrett.

Ms. Tweet sighed. "I saw Priscilla beside her bike, never on it."

"I can't give you a license, Priscilla. Not until you get a bigger bike."

"I told you that old bike was too small for me," said Priscilla the next afternoon. She watched Mr. Robin unstrap the new bike from the car's bike rack.

"*Too babyish* is what you said. If you had said *too small,* I would have paid attention. I thought you were letting Felicity get you down." Mr. Robin set the new bike in the driveway. It was tall, shiny, and black with narrow tires.

"Pretty snazzy," said Mrs. Robin.

Eve circled it and nodded. "When she sees it, Felicity will be steamed!"

"Felicity already has seen it," said Priscilla. With a corner of her sweater she rubbed Eve's and Mr. Robin's fingerprints off the handlebars.

"Felicity was in the cycle shop when we got there," said Mr. Robin. His voice sounded squeaky as though he were trying not to laugh. "She was asking about blocks."

"Felicity won't use blocks. Even *she* would be too embarrassed for that," said Eve. "She'll leave her bike in the garage until she grows into it."

"Not Felicity!" Priscilla pointed to the street.

Up rode Felicity on the giant pink bike. She was seated, not standing. As she pedaled, two giant purple and gold blocks swirled around-around-around.

Like tops, thought Priscilla. Like Fourth of July sparklers—

"They glow in the dark," yelled Felicity. "When I

go fast, sirens inside them squeal. They cost lots of money. Hey Priscilla, don't you wish you had a pair?"

Mr. Robin looked at Priscilla. So did Mrs. Robin. Pow-wow looked at Priscilla. So did Eve.

Priscilla said, "They glow in the dark?"

Felicity nodded.

"They have sirens that squeal?"

"Like a police car," said Felicity.

"Just how much did they cost?" said Priscilla.

Felicity fluffed her ruffles. "More money than you have. You wish you had some, don't you?"

Priscilla looked at her new bike with its narrow tires, its hand brakes, and its plain black pedals.

"Don't you?" said Felicity.

Priscilla stroked a shiny black fender. "No," she said. "I don't."